First U.S. edition 2009

Library of Congress Cataloging-in-Publication Data is available.
Library of Congress Catalog Card Number 2008938417
ISBN 978-0-7636-4420-8

2 4 6 8 10 9 7 5 3

Printed in China

This book was typeset in Latienne Swash.
The illustrations were done in pencil and acrylic.

Candlewick Press
99 Dover Street
Somerville, Massachusetts 02144

visit us at www.candlewick.com

NOT LAST NIGHT
BUT THE NIGHT BEFORE

Colin M^{*c*}*Naughton*

illustrated by **Emma Chichester Clark**

CANDLEWICK PRESS

For Coline and Gabin
C. M.

For William and Peter
E. C. C.

Not last night but the night before,
Three black cats came knocking at the door.

I came downstairs to let them in;
They knocked me down like a bowling pin.

Not last night but the night before,
The man in the moon came knocking at the door.

He rushed right in; he didn't stop.

He spun me round like a spinning top.

Not last night but the night before,
Three little pigs came knocking at the door.

They roared right in like a choo-choo train
And knocked me down on my back again.

Not last night but the night before,
Little Bo-peep came knocking at the door.

Goodness gracious, fancy that.
She darted in and knocked me flat.

(She'd found her sheep.)

Not last night but the night before,
Little Miss Muffet came knocking at the door.

I opened the door—she opened it wider,
And I got squished by a big fat spider.

Not last night but the night before,
Jack and Jill came knocking at the door.

Jack rolled in and shrieked with laughter;
Sister Jill came tumbling after.

Not last night but the night before,
Three blind mice came knocking at the door.

The farmer's wife, oh fiddle-dee-dee!

I saw her but she didn't see me.

(See how they run!)

Not last night but the night before,
Goldilocks came knocking at the door.

I thought that she'd come on her own.

Crash! Bang! Wallop! Well, I might have known.

Not last night but the night before,
Mister Punch came knocking at the door.

Judy, Baby, and Crocodile too,

Said, "Good evening. How do you do?"

(Now that's the way to do it!)

Not last night but the night before,

There was no more knocking on my door.

A glass was tapped—*ting, ting, ting!*

And all of a sudden they began to sing . . .

"Happy birthday to you,

Squashed tomatoes and stew,

Bread and butter in the gutter,

Happy birthday to you!"

Not last night but the night before,

I spread my gifts on the bedroom floor.

The house was still; there wasn't a peep.

I went to bed and I fell asleep!